# *The Berenstain Bears*

# Brother Bear
# Favorites

**3 Books in 1**

written by
Jan & Mike Berenstain

ZONDERKIDZ

*The Berenstain Bears Brother Bear Favorites*
Copyright © 2019 by Berenstain Publishing, Inc.
Illustrations © 2019 by Berenstain Publishing, Inc.

Requests for information should be addressed to:
Zonderkidz, 3900 *Sparks Dr. SE, Grand Rapids, Michigan* 49546

Hardcover ISBN  978-0-310-76913-2
Ebook ISBN 978-0-310-76914-9

*The Berenstain Bears® The Forgiving Tree* ISBN 9780310720843 (2010)
*The Berenstain Bears® Get Involved* ISBN 9780310720904 (2012)
*The Berenstain Bears® and A Job Well Done* ISBN 9780310712541 (2010)

*Art direction: Diane Mielke*

Printed in China

19  20  21  22  23  24 /DSC/ 10  9  8  7  6  5  4  3  2  1

# The Berenstain Bears

# The FORGIVING TREE

Living Lights™
A Faith Story

HAPPY BIRTHDAY BROTHER BEAR!

"For if you forgive men when they sin against you,
your heavenly Father will also forgive you."

—Matthew 6:14

ZONDERkidz

It was a special day in a tree house down a sunny dirt road deep in Bear Country. It was Brother Bear's birthday.

"Happy Birthday, Brother!" shouted the party guests as Mama brought in the cake. Then they all sang the birthday song.

"Make a wish!" said Sister.
Brother closed his eyes, made a wish, and blew out the candles.
"YEA!" the guests yelled, clapping and blowing on noisemakers.

Papa cut the cake and everyone dug in.
"What did you wish for?" asked Cousin Fred.
"If I tell, it won't come true," said Brother.

When they were finished eating the cake, it was time to open presents. Brother got some very nice ones—a model plane, some books, a racing car set, and a video game.

Then he noticed Papa sneaking into the next room. When he came back, he was pushing ... *a brand-new bike!*

"Wow!" said Brother excitedly. "It's exactly what I wished for!"

"Lucky you didn't tell Fred," said Sister.

"That's a beautiful bike," said Fred, admiring it. "I sure wish I had a bike like that."

"Oh," said Brother, without thinking, "you can borrow it anytime you like."

"Gee, thanks!" said Fred.

"Let's try out your new video game," suggested Sister.

All the cubs crowded around while Brother and Sister played the new video game. They were so interested, they didn't notice anything else for awhile. But then Brother looked over at his brand-new bike. It was gone!

"Hey!" said Brother. "Where's my new bike?"

"Say," said Lizzy, looking out the window, "isn't that Fred riding it?"

Lizzy was right. Cousin Fred was outside riding Brother's brand-new bike around the tree house. Brother was furious!

"That Fred!" growled Brother. "He can't do that!" And he
charged outside.

"Uh-oh!" said Mama and Papa, running after him.

But they were too late. Brother was already chasing Fred around the tree house yelling for him to get off his bike. He startled Fred so much that poor Fred didn't look where he was going and ran right into the mailbox.

He wasn't hurt, but the bike was. The front wheel was bent and wouldn't turn.

"Look what you did!" shouted Brother. "Who said you could ride my new bike?"

"*You* did," said Fred. "You said I could borrow it anytime."

"I didn't mean right away," said Brother, stamping his feet. "I never even got to ride it!"

"Now Brother," said Mama, "calm down. This is just a misunderstanding. Fred didn't mean any harm."

"But my bike is ruined!" cried Brother. "Just look at it!"

"It's not ruined," said Papa. "We'll take it down to the bike shop and get it fixed up as good as new."

"But it won't be new!" said Brother. "It will never be brand-new again!" And he stormed off in a huff.

"Gee, I'm sorry," said Fred. He felt awful. "I never meant to hurt Brother or his new bike."

"Of course not, Fred," soothed Mama. "It was just an accident."

"I'm sorry Brother's so mad," said Fred. "Do you think he'll ever forgive me?"

"Of course he will," said Papa. "He'll get over it in no time."

But Sister wasn't so sure. She followed Brother to their backyard tree house.

"Mind if I come up?" she called. Brother didn't answer. Sister climbed the ladder and found Brother sitting, sulking, at the top.

"You're certainly in a good mood," said Sister.

"Humph!" grunted Brother.

Sister noticed a faded red line drawn down the middle of the tree house floor.

"Do you remember this red line?" she asked.

Brother shrugged.

"We put it there a long time ago," Sister went on. "We were so mad at each other that we divided the tree house in half. I sat on one side, and you sat on the other. We sat out here being mad at each other until it started to rain and we got soaked. By that time, we couldn't even remember what we were mad about."

"I guess so," said Brother.

As Brother and Sister sat in their tree house, it became cloudy and started to rain. They went back to the party and found the guests getting ready to break the piñata.

It was one Papa made in his workshop. There were all kinds of candies inside but especially licorice because licorice was Papa's favorite. Papa held the piñata out on a broomstick.

"Okay," he said. "Start swinging. But be careful not to hit *me*!"

One after another, the cubs whacked the piñata until it finally broke open, spilling candy onto the floor.

They all scrambled to grab some, including Papa. Brother scrambled right into Fred. In fact, they knocked heads.

"Ow!" said Fred, rubbing his noggin.

"Oops, sorry!" said Brother.

"That's okay, Brother," said Fred. "I forgive you."

"I forgive you too, Fred," said Brother, feeling ashamed of himself. "I shouldn't have yelled at you about the bike. It really was just an accident."

"Forget it," said Fred … and forget it they did as they gathered up the candy.

"You know," said Papa to Mama, as they watched the happy cubs, "that old tree in the backyard has seen a lot of forgiving over the years. I guess you'd call it a Forgiving Tree."

"As the Lord said," smiled Mama:
"And forgive us our debts, as we forgive
our debtors."

"What does that mean?" asked Sister.

"Just that God wants us to forgive those who hurt our feelings," said Mama.

"And, remember," added Papa, "though God wants us to be good, he forgives us when we do something wrong."

"Well, I think that's very nice of God," said Sister.
"Yes," agreed Mama and Papa, "it is!"

# The Berenstain Bears®
# Get Involved

written by
Jan & Mike Berenstain

Living Lights™
A Faith Story

ZONDER**kidz**

Brother and Sister Bear belonged to the Cub Club at the Chapel in the Woods. Preacher Brown was their leader. They did lots of fun things together. They went on picnics,

played baseball

and basketball,

sang in the chorus,
        put on plays, painted
            pictures of Bible stories,

and put up decorations in the
chapel at Christmastime.

But the Cub Club was about
much more than just doing fun
things.

The real purpose of the club was to help others. There was always something that needed to be done around Bear Country. Sometimes it was cleaning up the Beartown playground.

Sometimes it was bringing food to bears who couldn't get out and about.

Sometimes it was even fixing up old houses for folks who couldn't fix them up themselves.

Brother and Sister liked to be helpful. It made them feel good deep down inside. Preacher Brown explained that it was always a good thing to help those in need.

"As the Bible says," he told them, "'Whoever is kind to the needy honors God.'"

So the Cub Club went right on helping others all over Bear Country.

Little did they know that very soon their help would be truly needed indeed!

One morning at breakfast, Papa Bear was reading the weather forecast.

"Says here it will rain for the next two days," he said. "Rain, rain, and more rain!"

"Oh, dear," said Mama. "I was planning to do laundry and air it out on the line. It will have to wait."

Brother and Sister didn't pay much attention. A little rain didn't seem to be anything to get very excited about.

On the way to school,
Brother and Sister noticed the
sky growing very dark.

By the time they
reached school, it was
starting to drizzle.

Through the morning, it rained harder and harder. It rained so hard that recess was cancelled and they had a study period instead.

"Phooey on rain!" muttered Brother.

"Rain, rain, go away," recited Sister. "Come again some other day."

But the rain paid no attention. It came pouring down harder than ever.

"I think you made it worse," said Brother.

When school let out, the cubs splashed their way home through the puddles. But then they heard a car coming down the road. It was Mama. She was coming to pick them up.

"Thanks, Mama," said the cubs. "We were getting soaked!"

Back home, Papa had a fire going in the fireplace, and Mama spread their wet clothes out to dry. Brother and Sister played with Honey in front of the cozy fire.

"This rain is getting serious," said Papa. "There could be flooding along the river."

"Oh, dear!" said Mama. "That's where Uncle Ned, Aunt Min, and Cousin Fred live. I do hope they don't get flooded out."

Brother and Sister pricked up their ears. What would it mean if Cousin Fred's family got "flooded out"?

At bedtime, Brother and Sister could hear the wind howling and the rain beating against the windows. It was a little spooky, but they snuggled down under the covers and soon drifted off to sleep.

They dreamed about
rushing streams

and roaring waterfalls.

It was still raining when they woke up the next morning.

"Wow!" said Brother, pressing against the windowpane. "Look at it coming down!"

As Brother and Sister went downstairs, they heard Papa on the phone.

"Don't worry," he said. "I'll be right over!"

"Over where?" asked Mama.

"That was Preacher Brown," said Papa, getting his coat and hat. "The river is rising fast, and we'll need to get everyone out of their houses down there. We're meeting at the chapel."

"We'll all come with you," said Mama. "There'll be plenty for everyone to do."

Brother and Sister were excited. They had never been part of a rescue mission before.

At the Chapel in the Woods, bears were gathering from all over. Their cars were loaded with shovels and buckets, bundles of blankets, and boxes of food. Grizzly Gus had a load of sandbags in his truck.

Preacher Brown saw Brother, Sister, and some of the other cubs. "I want all you Cub Club members to go along with your dads and help out," he told them. "This is what the Cub Club is all about!"

"Yes, sir!" they said. They were glad to be going. And Brother and Sister especially wanted to make sure Cousin Fred was all right.

The cars drove through the storm, down to the river.

"We're just in time," said Papa. "The water is nearly up to the houses."

An angry river was swirling over its banks and lapping toward
the houses.

"Look! There's Cousin Fred!" said Sister.

Cousin Fred, with Uncle Ned and Aunt Min, was leaning out of
an upstairs window and waving.

The bears all set to work piling up sandbags and digging ditches to keep the water away from the houses. Brother, Sister, Cousin Fred, and the rest of the Cub Club joined in. They dug and dug and dug until they were cold, wet, and tired.

Then everyone drove back to the chapel to warm up, dry off, and get something to eat.

Preacher Brown's wife, along with Mama and the other moms, had soup and sandwiches ready for all those cold, wet bears. They wrapped them in dry blankets and settled them down in the chapel's pews. Miz McGrizz sat at the organ to give them a little music.

"I'm so glad you're all right!" said Mama to Uncle Ned, Aunt Min, and Cousin Fred, giving them big hugs and kisses.

Preacher Brown got up in the pulpit, opened the Bible, and started to read: "The floodgates of the heavens were opened. And rain fell on the earth … The waters flooded the earth …"

Sister noticed a bright light coming through the chapel windows.

"Look!" she said. "The rain is stopping, and the sun is coming out!"

"The rain had stopped falling from the sky," read Preacher Brown.

"And there's a rainbow!"
said Brother.

"I have set my rainbow in the
clouds, ... " Preacher Brown read,
and closed the Bible.

"With God's help, we are all safe and sound," said Preacher Brown. "Thanks to everyone for pitching in and helping out. I particularly want to thank our youngest helpers, the members of the Cub Club."

All the bears clapped for Brother, Sister, Cousin Fred, and the Cub Club. They had been there to help others when their help was truly needed.

# The Berenstain Bears
## and A Job Well Done

written by
Jan and Mike Berenstain

Living Lights™ A Faith Story

ZONDERkidz

It was spring in Bear Country. And that meant that it was
spring cleaning and fix-up time at the Bear family's tree house.
Mama, Papa, Brother, Sister, and even Honey all had jobs to do.

Mama and Papa got right down to work. Mama hung up rugs on the line to beat the dirt out of them. Papa started to fix the broken railing on the front steps.

Brother and Sister had a job too. They were supposed to clean up the old playhouse in the backyard. Honey was going to help them.

They all got off to a good start. The sun was shining, and the air was fresh and clean. Birds were singing, and bright flowers were blooming in the garden.

Mama whacked at the rugs. Huge clouds of dirt flew out of them.

Papa's tools were everywhere. He knelt down to carve a piece of wood into the right shape for the railing.

Brother, Sister, and Honey had everything they needed for their job. They had brooms and brushes, cloths and mops, buckets of hot water and lots of soap. First, they were going to sweep out the inside of the playhouse.

"Uh-oh!" said Brother, looking inside the playhouse. "Spiders!"

Sister and Honey peeked inside. Sure enough, there were some big, hairy spiders sitting in their webs up in the corners of the playhouse. Brother, Sister, and Honey hated spiders!

"Yuck!" they all said.

"What should we do?" asked Sister.

"Let's not sweep out the inside," said Brother. "Let's scrub the outside. Maybe that will scare the spiders out."

That's what they did. Brother worked his way around the playhouse with his scrub brush, whistling while he worked.

"Hey, look!" he said when he got to the back. "We left some baseball stuff out here."

There was an old baseball, a bat, and a glove behind the playhouse.

Brother picked up the ball, tossed it in the air, and caught it. Sister picked up the bat and gave it a few swings.

"Pitch it in!" she said to Brother.

Brother wound up and tossed the ball to Sister. She swatted it across the lawn.

"Here, Honey," said Brother, giving her the glove. "You be the outfielder."

Honey toddled out into the lawn and sat down.

Meanwhile, back at the tree house, Mama and Papa were hard at work. Mama was nearly done with the rugs. She was absolutely covered with dirt.

Papa was nearly finished with the railing. He fastened the wood in place, then straightened up and stretched.

That's when Papa noticed
Honey sitting in the middle
of the lawn. He couldn't see
Brother or Sister. They were
behind the tree house.
    "What is Honey
doing just sitting there?"
wondered Papa.

A baseball came sailing into sight and landed near Honey. She grabbed it and threw it back.

"Hmmm!" said Papa, rubbing his chin.

Papa walked around the tree house and saw Brother and Sister playing baseball. Their brooms, brushes, cloths, and mops were all lying on the ground.

Papa stood behind Brother and Sister.

"Baseball is a fine springtime activity," he said, "but so is spring cleaning!"

Brother and Sister spun around and hid the ball and bat behind their backs.

"Oh, hi, Papa!" they both grinned. "We were just taking a little break."

Papa looked into the very dirty playhouse.

"It looks like you've been taking a *big* break," he said. "You've hardly touched this playhouse."

"But Papa," started Brother.

"There are lots of spiders in there!" finished Sister.

Papa smiled. He remembered how scared he was of spiders when he was a cub. He still didn't like them very much. "Well," he said, "I'll chase the spiders out for you. But, then, you need to get the job done."

Papa chased the spiders out of the playhouse with a broom. They ran off and hid in the storage shed, which was a better home for them, anyway.

Then, Brother, Sister, and Honey went back to work.

"Did you know that the Bible has something to say about working hard and getting the job done?" asked Papa as they cleaned.

"No," said Brother.

"What does it say?" said Sister.

"It says," said Papa, "'finish your outdoor work and get your fields ready; after that, build your house.'"

"Did you build a house today, Papa?" asked Sister.

"Well," said Papa, proudly, "I built a new railing."

"And," added Mama, who had come up to see what was going on, "it says in the Bible that God made work for us to do and there's nothing better than to enjoy your work."

"Did you enjoy your work, Mama?" asked Brother.

Mama rubbed some of the dirt off her face. "Well," she said, "I enjoy my clean rugs—and you will enjoy your clean playhouse."

"Especially without all those spiders!" agreed Sister.
"Yuck!" said Honey.
Mama, Papa, Brother, and Sister all laughed.

# Activities and Questions from Brother and Sister Bear

Talk about it:

1. Would you have done the same thing as Brother and offered to share your bike with Cousin Fred? Why?

2. Would you have been as upset as Brother if someone that you care about had an accident with something that was yours? What might you do differently?

3. How was Sister a help to Brother?

4. Why is it sometimes very hard to say you are sorry and also hard to accept an apology?

Get out and do it:

1. On a large sheet of butcher paper, design a Family Forgiving Tree. Have an envelope filled with cut-outs of leaves near where you hang the tree. When you need to say you are sorry to someone, write about it on a leaf and tape it to the tree. It feels good to ask for forgiveness and to be forgiven!

# Activities and Questions from Brother and Sister Bear

Talk about it:

1. What types of things did the Cub Club usually do for the Bear community? Does the youth group or Sunday school at your church do any of the same activities and service projects?

2. Why did many of the bears of Bear Country gather at the Chapel in the Woods?

3. Why do you think Brother and Sister are especially interested in helping out during the big rains?

Get out and do it:

1. As a family, get involved in a community or church project. Help collect food items for a food drive or blankets for a blanket collection. Organize a bake sale, and donate the funds to a local charity or to your church's service organization or mission.

2. Getting involved can be as simple as making cards for neighborhood shut-ins or people from your church that are in the hospital or a nursing home. Gather some of your friends and make cards or write letters that give encouragement and hope to others.

# Activities and Questions from Brother and Sister Bear

Talk about it:

1. Do you have at-home jobs that need to get done before you can have some fun? Name some of the chores you do and how it helps the family when you finish them completely.

2. What do you think Papa Bear meant when he said the Bible says, "finish your outdoor work and get your fields ready; after that, build your house?"

Get out and do it:

1. Design a family chore chart. Hang the chart up and check it daily, making sure you are completing your family responsibilities.

2. Help someone in your family with one of their given jobs around the house. Do not wait to be asked!